Dedication

In solemn remembrance and heartfelt tribute, this book is dedicated to the over 10,000 Palestinian Children massacred by merciless onslaught of the Israeli military of the Palestinian people in the Genocide of Gaza during just the first 100 days. Their innocent lives, marked by unwarranted suffering and unimaginable loss, serve as a poignant reminder of the profound human cost of conflict.

May the collective cry's of these young innocent Children echo through the pages of this book, resonating across the globe, and inspiring a universal call for a stop to all wars, violence and all people's of earth to live in peace. In dedicating these words to the precious lives murdered, we aspire to ignite a transformative conversation about the imperative need to abandon violence as a means of resolving our differences.

May the memories of the Palestinian children be a catalyst for change, motivating people worldwide to seek paths to dialogue, diplomacy, and comprehensive peace with each other. In their honor, let us unite in our commitment to building a world where conflicts are resolved through courts of law, cooperation, and a shared vision of peaceful coexistence. May their legacy be a guiding light, urging us all to work tirelessly towards a future where every child can grow and thrive in a world free from the shadows of violence and war.

PEOPLEIZE

Chapter 2

Government By The People: Decolonizing Governmental System

The Day After
The Genocide In Gaza For Earth

By Einar Ourlove

PEOPLEIZE

This is a work of fiction. All of the characters, organizations, and events portrayed in this novel are either products of the author's imagination and are being used fictitiously in this novel.

Copyright ©

All rights reserved.

Our books may be purchased in bulk for promotional, educational, or business use. Please contact your local bookseller or us directly at info@einarourlove.com

www.einarourlove.com
www.peopleize.world

Originally published 2024

Contents

Chapter i

Decolonizing Government

In a world where governance profoundly influences the daily existence of billions, it's crucial to examine the systems in place through a lens that considers the fundamental needs crucial for human survival. These essential needs encompass **water, food, shelter, clothing, and healthcare,** forming the cornerstone of well-being and vitality for individuals worldwide.

Water stands as a vital element for sustaining life, serving as a fundamental necessity for hydration, supporting bodily functions, and promoting overall health. Yet, access to clean and safe drinking water remains a challenge for many, highlighting a critical gap in governance efforts to ensure basic needs are met.

Similarly, nutritious **food** is indispensable for providing the energy and essential nutrients necessary for proper bodily function. Agriculture plays a pivotal role in this regard, yet disparities in food security persist, underscoring the failure of governance systems to ensure equitable access to sustenance for all citizens.

Shelter offers more than mere protection from the elements; it provides a sanctuary where individuals can seek refuge and find respite. However, housing insecurity and homelessness persist in many regions, revealing a systemic failure to address the basic need for secure and stable shelter.

Clothing, essential for safeguarding individuals against environmental factors and regulating body temperature, is often taken for granted. Yet, access to adequate clothing remains a challenge for marginalized populations, highlighting gaps in governance efforts to ensure basic necessities are met for all citizens.

Access to comprehensive **healthcare** services is paramount for maintaining and promoting overall health. Despite advances in medical science, disparities in healthcare access persist globally, reflecting systemic failures in governance to provide equitable healthcare services for all citizens.

In a world where governance shapes the lives of billions, it's imperative to scrutinize the systems in place through a holistic lens that considers the fulfillment of these fundamental human needs. From autocracies to democracies, the spectrum of governance is vast, yet the ability of these systems to effectively address the basic needs of their citizens remains a critical measure of their success and legitimacy.

These estimates show the scale of the failure of the USA government over the last 200 years to provide the basic needs for its population.

1. **Access to Clean Water:** While the United States generally has a well-developed infrastructure for clean water delivery, there are still significant challenges. Estimates suggest that millions of Americans, particularly in rural or impoverished areas, lack access to safe and clean drinking water. The Flint water crisis in Michigan, for instance, affected approximately 100,000 residents. It is just one of many examples.

2. **Food Security:** Despite being one of the world's largest food producers, food insecurity affects millions of Americans. It's estimated that over 38 million people, including children, experience hunger or food insecurity in the United States. This includes individuals living in poverty, those in food deserts, and those who face barriers to accessing government assistance programs like SNAP (Supplemental Nutrition Assistance Program) or WIC (Special Supplemental Nutrition Program for Women, Infants, and Children).

3. **Housing Insecurity:** Homelessness and housing insecurity are significant issues in the United States. Estimates indicate that on any given night, over half a million Americans experience homelessness. Additionally, many more individuals and families face housing

insecurity, uncertain about their ability to afford rent or housing costs.

4. **Healthcare Access:** Despite efforts to expand healthcare coverage through initiatives like the Affordable Care Act (ACA), significant gaps in healthcare access persist. It's estimated that over 30 million Americans remain uninsured, and many more face barriers to accessing quality healthcare due to factors such as high healthcare costs, limited availability of healthcare facilities, and disparities in healthcare outcomes based on race and socioeconomic status.

5. **Clothing and Basic Necessities:** While access to clothing may not be as widespread an issue as access to food, water, shelter, and healthcare, there are still vulnerable populations struggling to obtain adequate clothing and basic necessities. It's difficult to estimate the exact number of individuals affected, but it includes homeless populations, refugees, and those living in poverty, which collectively amount to millions of people across the United States.

Looking at the UN we see that these estimates shows the significant failure by United Nations to provide for the Earth people the basic needs:

1. **Access to Clean Water:** Globally, an estimated 2.2 billion people lack access to safely managed drinking water services, and

around 4.2 billion people experience severe water scarcity at least one month a year. The United Nations, through its Sustainable Development Goals (SDGs), particularly Goal 6: Clean Water and Sanitation, aims to ensure universal access to safe and affordable drinking water for all by 2030.

2. **Food Security:** Approximately 690 million people worldwide suffer from hunger, with the majority living in developing regions. The UN's Food and Agriculture Organization (FAO) works to eliminate hunger and malnutrition through initiatives such as the Zero Hunger Challenge, which seeks to ensure access to safe and nutritious food for all.

3. **Housing Insecurity:** The UN estimates that over 1.6 billion people worldwide lack adequate housing, with slum populations expected to exceed 1 billion by 2030 if current trends continue. The UN's New Urban Agenda and Sustainable Development Goal 11: Sustainable Cities and Communities aim to ensure access to adequate, safe, and affordable housing for all, particularly the urban poor.

4. **Healthcare Access:** The World Health Organization (WHO) estimates that at least half of the world's population still lacks access to essential health services, and millions suffer financial hardship due to out-of-pocket healthcare expenses. The UN's Sustainable

Development Goal 3: Good Health and Well-being seeks to ensure healthy lives and promote well-being for all at all ages, including universal health coverage.

5. **Clothing and Basic Necessities:** While access to clothing and basic necessities is not explicitly addressed by a specific UN goal, it is often intertwined with broader issues of poverty and inequality. The UN's work in promoting sustainable development, poverty alleviation, and social protection aims to address the underlying factors that contribute to lack of access to clothing and basic necessities for vulnerable populations.

Looking at the list of 195 global counties on Earth we see their governments are presented by the old colonial system of having just one head and not representing all the people equally:

1. Afghanistan: Presidential Republic (President)
2. Albania: Parliamentary Republic (President)
3. Algeria: Presidential Republic (President)
4. Andorra: Parliamentary Democracy (Co-Princes)
5. Angola: Presidential Republic (President)
6. Antigua and Barbuda: Constitutional Monarchy (Monarch) and Parliamentary Democracy (Prime Minister)
7. Argentina: Presidential Republic (President)

8. Armenia: Semi-Presidential Republic (Prime Minister and President)
9. Australia: Federal Parliamentary Democracy (Monarch and Prime Minister)
10. Austria: Federal Parliamentary Republic (Federal President)
11. Azerbaijan: Presidential Republic (President)
12. Bahamas: Constitutional Monarchy (Monarch) and Parliamentary Democracy (Prime Minister)
13. Bahrain: Constitutional Monarchy (King) and Parliamentary Democracy (Prime Minister)
14. Bangladesh: Parliamentary Republic (President)
15. Barbados: Constitutional Monarchy (Monarch) and Parliamentary Democracy (Prime Minister)
16. Belarus: Presidential Republic (President)
17. Belgium: Federal Parliamentary Democracy (Monarch and Prime Minister)
18. Belize: Constitutional Monarchy (Monarch) and Parliamentary Democracy (Prime Minister)
19. Benin: Presidential Republic (President)
20. Bhutan: Constitutional Monarchy (King)
21. Bolivia: Presidential Republic (President)
22. Bosnia and Herzegovina: Federal Parliamentary Republic (Presidency)
23. Botswana: Parliamentary Republic (President)
24. Brazil: Federal Presidential Republic (President)

25. Brunei: Absolute Monarchy (Sultan)
26. Bulgaria: Parliamentary Republic (Prime Minister)
27. Burkina Faso: Presidential Republic (President)
28. Burundi: Presidential Republic (President)
29. Cabo Verde: Semi-Presidential Republic (President and Prime Minister)
30. Cambodia: Constitutional Monarchy (King) and Parliamentary Democracy (Prime Minister)
31. Cameroon: Presidential Republic (President)
32. Canada: Federal Parliamentary Democracy (Monarch and Prime Minister)
33. Central African Republic: Presidential Republic (President)
34. Chad: Presidential Republic (President)
35. Chile: Presidential Republic (President)
36. China: One-Party Socialist Republic (President)
37. Colombia: Presidential Republic (President)
38. Comoros: Federal Presidential Republic (President)
39. Democratic Republic of the Congo: Semi-Presidential Republic (President and Prime Minister)
40. Republic of the Congo: Presidential Republic (President)
41. Costa Rica: Presidential Republic (President)
42. Croatia: Parliamentary Republic (President)

43. Cuba: One-Party Socialist Republic (President)
44. Cyprus: Presidential Republic (President)
45. Czech Republic: Parliamentary Republic (President)
46. Denmark: Constitutional Monarchy (Monarch) and Parliamentary Democracy (Prime Minister)
47. Djibouti: Presidential Republic (President)
48. Dominica: Parliamentary Democracy (President and Prime Minister)
49. Dominican Republic: Presidential Republic (President)
50. East Timor (Timor-Leste): Semi-Presidential Republic (President and Prime Minister)
51. Ecuador: Presidential Republic (President)
52. Egypt: Presidential Republic (President)
53. El Salvador: Presidential Republic (President)
54. Equatorial Guinea: Presidential Republic (President)
55. Eritrea: One-Party State (President)
56. Estonia: Parliamentary Republic (President)
57. Eswatini: Absolute Monarchy (King)
58. Ethiopia: Federal Parliamentary Republic (President)
59. Fiji: Parliamentary Republic (President and Prime Minister)
60. Finland: Parliamentary Republic (President)

61. France: Semi-Presidential Republic (President and Prime Minister)
62. Gabon: Presidential Republic (President)
63. Gambia: Presidential Republic (President)
64. Georgia: Semi-Presidential Republic (President and Prime Minister)
65. Germany: Federal Parliamentary Republic (Federal President and Chancellor)
66. Ghana: Presidential Republic (President)
67. Greece: Parliamentary Republic (President)
68. Grenada: Constitutional Monarchy (Monarch) and Parliamentary Democracy (Prime Minister)
69. Guatemala: Presidential Republic (President)
70. Guinea: Presidential Republic (President)
71. Guinea-Bissau: Semi-Presidential Republic (President and Prime Minister)
72. Guyana: Presidential Republic (President)
73. Haiti: Semi-Presidential Republic (President and Prime Minister)
74. Honduras: Presidential Republic (President)
75. Hungary: Parliamentary Republic (Prime Minister)
76. Iceland: Parliamentary Republic (President)
77. India: Federal Parliamentary Republic (President and Prime Minister)
78. Indonesia: Presidential Republic (President)
79. Iran: Islamic Republic (Supreme Leader and President)

80. Iraq: Federal Parliamentary Republic (President and Prime Minister)
81. Ireland: Parliamentary Republic (President and Taoiseach)
82. Israel: Parliamentary Republic (President and Prime Minister)
83. Italy: Parliamentary Republic (President and Prime Minister)
84. Jamaica: Constitutional Monarchy (Monarch) and Parliamentary Democracy (Prime Minister)
85. Japan: Parliamentary Constitutional Monarchy (Emperor and Prime Minister)
86. Jordan: Constitutional Monarchy (King) and Parliamentary Democracy (Prime Minister)
87. Kazakhstan: Presidential Republic (President)
88. Kenya: Presidential Republic (President)
89. Kiribati: Parliamentary Republic (President and Prime Minister)
90. North Korea: One-Party Socialist Republic (Supreme Leader)
91. South Korea: Presidential Republic (President)
92. Kosovo: Parliamentary Republic (President and Prime Minister)
93. Kuwait: Constitutional Monarchy (Emir) and Parliamentary Democracy (Prime Minister)
94. Kyrgyzstan: Presidential Republic (President)
95. Laos: One-Party Socialist Republic (President)

96. Latvia: Parliamentary Republic (President)
97. Lebanon: Parliamentary Republic (President and Prime Minister)
98. Lesotho: Parliamentary Constitutional Monarchy (King and Prime Minister)
99. Liberia: Presidential Republic (President)
100. Libya: Transitional Government (Chairman of the Presidential Council)
101. Liechtenstein: Constitutional Monarchy (Prince) and Parliamentary Democracy (Prime Minister)
102. Lithuania: Parliamentary Republic (President)
103. Luxembourg: Parliamentary Constitutional Monarchy (Monarch and Prime Minister)
104. Madagascar: Semi-Presidential Republic (President and Prime Minister)
105. Malawi: Presidential Republic (President)
106. Malaysia: Constitutional Monarchy (King) and Parliamentary Democracy (Prime Minister)
107. Maldives: Presidential Republic (President)
108. Mali: Semi-Presidential Republic (President and Prime Minister)
109. Malta: Parliamentary Republic (President and Prime Minister)
110. Marshall Islands: Parliamentary Republic (President and President)
111. Mauritania: Presidential Republic (President)
112. Mauritius: Parliamentary Republic (President and Prime Minister)

113. Mexico: Federal Presidential Republic (President)
114. Micronesia: Presidential Republic (President and President)
115. Moldova: Parliamentary Republic (President and Prime Minister)
116. Monaco: Constitutional Monarchy (Prince) and Parliamentary Democracy (Minister of State)
117. Mongolia: Semi-Presidential Republic (President and Prime Minister)
118. Montenegro: Parliamentary Republic (President and Prime Minister)
119. Morocco: Constitutional Monarchy (King) and Parliamentary Democracy (Prime Minister)
120. Mozambique: Presidential Republic (President)
121. Myanmar (Burma): Presidential Republic (President)
122. Namibia: Presidential Republic (President)
123. Nauru: Parliamentary Republic (President and President)
124. Nepal: Federal Parliamentary Republic (President and Prime Minister)
125. Netherlands: Parliamentary Constitutional Monarchy (Monarch and Prime Minister)
126. New Zealand: Parliamentary Constitutional Monarchy (Monarch and Prime Minister)
127. Nicaragua: Presidential Republic (President)
128. Niger: Presidential Republic (President)

129. Nigeria: Federal Presidential Republic (President)
130. North Macedonia: Parliamentary Republic (President and Prime Minister)
131. Norway: Constitutional Monarchy (Monarch) and Parliamentary Democracy (Prime Minister)
132. Oman: Absolute Monarchy (Sultan)
133. Pakistan: Federal Parliamentary Republic (President and Prime Minister)
134. Palau: Presidential Republic (President and President)
135. Panama: Presidential Republic (President)
136. Papua New Guinea: Parliamentary Constitutional Monarchy (Monarch and Prime Minister)
137. Paraguay: Presidential Republic (President)
138. Peru: Presidential Republic (President)
139. Philippines: Presidential Republic (President)
140. Poland: Parliamentary Republic (President and Prime Minister)
141. Portugal: Parliamentary Republic (President and Prime Minister)
142. Qatar: Absolute Monarchy (Emir)
143. Romania: Semi-Presidential Republic (President and Prime Minister)
144. Russia: Presidential Republic (President)
145. Rwanda: Presidential Republic (President)

146. Saint Kitts and Nevis: Constitutional Monarchy (Monarch) and Parliamentary Democracy (Prime Minister)
147. Saint Lucia: Constitutional Monarchy (Monarch) and Parliamentary Democracy (Prime Minister)
148. Saint Vincent and the Grenadines: Constitutional Monarchy (Monarch) and Parliamentary Democracy (Prime Minister)
149. Samoa: Parliamentary Republic (Head of State and Prime Minister)
150. San Marino: Parliamentary Republic (Captains Regent)
151. Sao Tome and Principe: Semi-Presidential Republic (President and Prime Minister)
152. Saudi Arabia: Absolute Monarchy (King)
153. Senegal: Semi-Presidential Republic (President and Prime Minister)
154. Serbia: Parliamentary Republic (President and Prime Minister)
155. Seychelles: Presidential Republic (President)
156. Sierra Leone: Presidential Republic (President)
157. Singapore: Parliamentary Republic (President and Prime Minister)
158. Slovakia: Parliamentary Republic (President and Prime Minister)
159. Slovenia: Parliamentary Republic (President and Prime Minister)
160. Solomon Islands: Parliamentary Republic (Monarch and Prime Minister)

161. Somalia: Federal Parliamentary Republic (President and Prime Minister)
162. South Africa: Parliamentary Republic (President and President)
163. South Sudan: Presidential Republic (President)
164. Spain: Parliamentary Constitutional Monarchy (Monarch and Prime Minister)
165. Sri Lanka: Semi-Presidential Republic (President and Prime Minister)
166. Sudan: Transitional Government (Sovereignty Council and Prime Minister)
167. Suriname: Presidential Republic (President)
168. Sweden: Parliamentary Constitutional Monarchy (Monarch and Prime Minister)
169. Switzerland: Federal Parliamentary Republic (Federal Council)
170. Syria: Presidential Republic (President)
171. Taiwan: Semi-Presidential Republic (President and Prime Minister)
172. Tajikistan: Presidential Republic (President)
173. Tanzania: Presidential Republic (President)
174. Thailand: Constitutional Monarchy (King) and Parliamentary Democracy (Prime Minister)
175. Togo: Presidential Republic (President)
176. Tonga: Constitutional Monarchy (King) and Parliamentary Democracy (Prime Minister)
177. Trinidad and Tobago: Parliamentary Republic (President and Prime Minister)

178. Tunisia: Parliamentary Republic (President and Prime Minister)
179. Turkey: Presidential Republic (President)
180. Turkmenistan: Presidential Republic (President)
181. Tuvalu: Parliamentary Democracy (Monarch and Prime Minister)
182. Uganda: Presidential Republic (President)
183. Ukraine: Semi-Presidential Republic (President and Prime Minister)
184. United Arab Emirates: Federal Absolute Monarchy (President and Prime Minister)
185. United Kingdom: Parliamentary Constitutional Monarchy (Monarch and Prime Minister)
186. United States: Federal Presidential Republic (President)
187. Uruguay: Presidential Republic (President)
188. Uzbekistan: Presidential Republic (President)
189. Vanuatu: Parliamentary Republic (President and Prime Minister)
190. Vatican City: Ecclesiastical Elective Monarchy (Pope)
191. Venezuela: Presidential Republic (President)
192. Vietnam: One-Party Socialist Republic (President)
193. Yemen: Provisional Government (President and Prime Minister)
194. Zambia: Presidential Republic (President)
195. Zimbabwe: Presidential Republic (President)

That is a total of **195 individuals** that control the lives of the **7.9 billion** people on earth. And as seen with the Genocide in Gaza, they can do what every they want without regard for the population of the world thinks even while allowing Genocide by Israel with their military and finical support.

A common thread emerges: the concentration of power in the hands of a select few. Regardless of the form of government, be it a monarchy, dictatorship, republic, or democracy, there's always an individual wielding ultimate authority. This figure, whether titled president, monarch, or prime minister, holds the reins of control over the populace.

Take the example of the Genocide on Gaza by Israel.

The United Nations General Assembly (UNGA) passed a resolution calling for a humanitarian ceasefire in war-torn Gaza with overwhelming support, receiving 153 votes in favor.

The 153 countries that voted in favor were: Afghanistan, Albania, Algeria, Andorra, Angola, Antigua and Barbuda, Armenia, Australia, Azerbaijan, Bahamas, Bahrain, Bangladesh, Barbados, Belarus, Belgium, Belize, Benin, Bhutan, Bolivia, Bosnia and Herzegovina, Botswana, Brazil, Brunei, Burundi, Cambodia, Canada, Central African Republic, Chad, Chile,

China, Colombia, Comoros, Costa Rica, Cote D'Ivoire, Croatia, Cuba, Cyprus, Democratic People's Republic of Korea (North Korea), Democratic Republic of the Congo, Denmark, Djibouti, Dominica, Dominican Republic, East Timor, Ecuador, Egypt, El Salvador, Eritrea, Estonia, Ethiopia, Fiji, Finland, France, Gabon, Gambia, Ghana, Greece, Grenada, Guinea, Guinea-Bissau, Guyana, Honduras, Iceland, India, Indonesia, Iran, Iraq, Ireland, Jamaica, Japan, Jordan, Kazakhstan, Kenya, Kuwait, Kyrgyzstan, Laos, Latvia, Lebanon, Lesotho, Libya, Liechtenstein, Luxembourg, Madagascar, Malaysia, Maldives, Mali, Malta, Mauritania, Mauritius, Mexico, Moldova, Monaco, Mongolia, Montenegro, Morocco, Mozambique, Myanmar, Namibia, Nepal, New Zealand, Nicaragua, Niger, Nigeria, North Macedonia, Norway, Oman, Pakistan, Peru, Philippines, Poland, Portugal, Qatar, Republic of Korea (South Korea), Russia, Rwanda, Republic of the Congo, Saint Kitts and Nevis, Saint Lucia, Saint Vincent and the Grenadines, Samoa, San Marino, Saudi Arabia, Senegal, Serbia, Seychelles, Sierra Leone, Singapore, Slovenia, Solomon Islands, Somalia, South Africa, Spain, Sri Lanka, Sudan, Suriname, Sweden, Switzerland, Syria, Tajikistan, Thailand, Trinidad and Tobago.

23 countries abstained from voting, including Argentina, Bulgaria, Cabo Verde, Cameroon, Equatorial Guinea, Georgia, Germany, Hungary, Italy, Lithuania, Malawi, Marshall Islands, Netherlands, Palau, Panama, Romania,

Slovakia, South Sudan, Togo, Tonga, Ukraine, United Kingdom, and Uruguay.

10 countries voted against the resolution, including Austria, Czech Republic, Guatemala, Israel, Liberia, Micronesia, Nauru, Papua New Guinea, Paraguay, and the United States.

In addition to the voting dynamics at the United Nations General Assembly (UNGA), it's crucial to consider the context surrounding the resolution on a humanitarian ceasefire in Gaza.

At the time of the vote, the Israeli military had already implemented a full blockade of Gaza, including cutting off all water, food, and essential supplies from entering the walled city of Gaza.

Furthermore, within the first 100 days of their war on Gaza, Israel military had confirmed   the massacres resulting from daily bombardments by the Israeli military, killing over 10,000 children. With total death toll of over 25,000 Palestinian's.

The International Court of Justice (ICJ) had already taken up the case, examining allegations of genocide against the Palestinian people in Gaza. And had issued an privative measures to ensure the stop of the Genocide while the case is heard.

Over the past 75 years, the ICJ had issued numerous decisions against Israel's illegal occupation of Palestinian territories, which have

have been disregarded by Israel and protected by the United States consistently vetoing any actions aimed at holding Israel accountable for these violations, highlighting a fundamental colonial mentality within the UN and the global power structures.

One clear example of this is the Genocide of Gaza by Israel on the indigenous Palestinian population:
As of February 16, 2024, Israel has continued its attacks across the Gaza Strip, including near hospitals and in the south of the besieged enclave, where ground operations are intensifying.

Here are the latest casualty figures as of February 16 at 1pm in Gaza:

Gaza

- Killed: at least 28,775 people, including more than:
- 12,300 children
- 8,400 women
- Injured: more than 68,552, including at least:
- 8,663 children
- 6,327 women
- Missing: more than 7,000

The latest figures from the Palestinian Ministry of Health in the occupied West Bank are as follows:

Occupied West Bank

- Killed: at least 395 people, including more than:
- 105 children
- Injured: more than 4,450

In Israel, officials revised the death toll down from 1,405 to 1,139.

Devastation across Gaza

According to the latest data from the UN's Office for the Coordination of Humanitarian Affairs (OCHA), the World Health Organization (WHO) and the Palestinian government as of February 13, Israeli attacks have damaged:

- More than half of Gaza's homes - 360,000 residential units have been destroyed or damaged
- 392 educational facilities
- 11 out of 35 hospitals are partially functioning
- 123 ambulances
- 267 places of worship

Nowhere safe to go

The Israeli army published an online map of the Gaza Strip on December 1, dividing the enclave into more than 600 numbered blocks. It asked Gaza's civilians to identify the block corresponding with their area of residence and evacuate when ordered.

However, leaflets ordering evacuations are inconsistent with online warnings, which has confused residents.

Furthermore, several Gaza residents have no reliable way to access the map with little access to electricity or the internet since the blockade of the 365sq-km (141sq-mile) strip has resulted in a collapse of telecommunications infrastructure.

Every hour in Gaza:

- 15 people are killed - six are children
- 35 people are injured
- 42 bombs are dropped*
- 12 buildings are destroyed

Based on the first six days of the war, according to the Israeli army

Journalists killed

As of February 16, at least 99 journalists, mostly Palestinians, have been killed since the Israel-Gaza war that began in October. According to the Committee to Protect Journalists (CPJ) and the International Federation of Journalists (IFJ), 92 Palestinian, three Lebanese and four Israeli journalists have been killed.

Sixteen years of Israeli blockade

The Gaza Strip has a population of about 2.3 million people living in one of the most densely populated areas in the world and is located between Israel and Egypt on the Mediterranean coast.

Since 2007, Israel has maintained strict control over Gaza's airspace and territorial waters and restricted the movement of goods and people in and out of Gaza.

Israeli Prime Minister Benjamin Netanyahu has threatened to turn Gaza into a "deserted island" and warned its residents to "leave now".

Despite the collective decision-making power of the UN General Assembly, the implementation of its resolutions often faces obstacles within the UN Security Council, primarily due to the veto authority held by certain permanent members, including the USA. This veto protection allows these nations to block any resolution they deem contrary to their national interests. As a result, even when a majority of UN member states support a measure, it may not be effectively implemented if it does not align with the preferences of the veto-wielding countries. Thus, the UN Security Council's ability to enforce decisions made by the General Assembly is significantly constrained, highlighting the challenges inherent in achieving consensus and effective global governance.

In this case the UN Security Council still cannot implement the vote of the UN General Assembly due to the veto protection of the USA.

This situation underscores the imbalance of power, with powerful military forces exerting control over less powerful nations and peoples. It serves as a stark reminder of the ongoing struggles faced by peaceful countries and communities that are now compelled to invest in their military capabilities to protect their governments against oppression and injustice, emphasizing the urgent need for equitable and just international governance. The current model of divide and conquer by force reflects a 2000-year-old colonial mentality that seeks to subjugate the people of the Earth under the dominance of the strongest military. This antiquated model must be stopped and changed.

This current trajectory could lead to a world where the wealthy reside in space above the Earth, while the 7.9 billion people on Earth toil to support their lifestyle in the skies above.

The analogy of the 400-meter race serves as a poignant metaphor for the inherent unfairness of the circumstances individuals find themselves born into. This visual depiction vividly portrays how factors like familial inheritance, birthplace, and socio-economic status dictate one's starting point in the race of life. At the core of PEOPLEIZE lies a fundamental belief: no human should lay claim to Earth or possess the authority to determine another's initial position in life's journey as a collective society.

When a person's outset is determined solely by the time, place, and lineage of their birth, the injustices perpetuated by the prevailing monetary system become starkly evident. Crafted by colonial powers indifferent to the local indigenous populations, this system ensures that a significant portion of the global community begins their lives at a disadvantage, with little hope of overcoming this systemic oppression.

Of the 195 countries existing today, 121 were established without consideration for the native inhabitants, their creation overseen by colonial powers that continue to manipulate monetary systems to maintain control. This manipulation ensures that future generations remain shackled by circumstances beyond their control, their potential stunted from birth without recourse. The list of nations born from European exploration, colonization, and settlement is extensive, each one leaving a legacy of exploitation and disregard for indigenous peoples.

These new nations, forged through land colonization, initially subjected indigenous populations to slavery before leveraging colonial treaties to exploit natural resources for European gain. Despite achieving independence, these countries continue to grapple with economic inequality and systematic marginalization of indigenous rights, perpetuating a cycle of oppression that endures to this day.

The 121 countries created without regard for indigenous populations include: United States, Canada, Mexico, Brazil, Argentina, Chile, Peru, Colombia, Venezuela, Bolivia, Uruguay, Paraguay, Ecuador, Australia, New Zealand, South Africa, Egypt, Algeria, Angola, Mozambique, Democratic Republic of the Congo, Republic of the Congo, Nigeria, Ghana, Kenya, Tanzania, South Sudan, Sudan, Ethiopia, Somalia, Morocco, Tunisia, Libya, Namibia, Botswana, Zimbabwe, Zambia, Malawi, Uganda, Rwanda, Burundi, Cameroon, Ivory Coast, Senegal, Guinea, Sierra Leone, Liberia, Gambia, Guinea-Bissau, Cape Verde, Mauritania, Western Sahara, Chad, Niger, Mali, Burkina Faso, Togo, Benin, Central African Republic, Gabon, Equatorial Guinea, Seychelles, Mauritius, Comoros, Madagascar, Maldives, Sri Lanka, Bangladesh, Myanmar, Malaysia, Indonesia, Philippines, Brunei, East Timor, India, Pakistan, Afghanistan, Nepal, Bhutan, Papua New Guinea, Solomon Islands, Fiji, Vanuatu, Samoa, Tonga, Tuvalu, Kiribati, Marshall Islands, Palau, Micronesia, Nauru, Cook Islands, Niue, Grenada, Saint Kitts and Nevis, Saint Lucia, Saint Vincent and the Grenadines, Antigua and Barbuda, Dominica, Bahamas, Barbados, Jamaica, Trinidad and Tobago, Guyana, Suriname, Belize, Haiti, Dominican Republic, Cuba, Costa Rica, Panama, El Salvador,

Honduras, Nicaragua, Guatemala, and Paraguay.

The United Nations (UN) structure creates additional challenges that impact its effectiveness in addressing global issues. One major issue is the imbalance of power and representation within its decision-making bodies, particularly the UN Security Council. The Security Council's five permanent members (the United States, Russia, China, France, and the United Kingdom) hold veto power, which can hinder decisive action on critical issues due to geopolitical interests and disagreements among these major powers.

Additionally, the distribution of seats in the General Assembly, where each member state has one vote regardless of size or population, can lead to disparities in influence and decision-making. This can result in the marginalization of smaller or less economically powerful countries, limiting their ability to shape international policies and agendas.

Moreover, the UN's bureaucracy and complex decision-making processes can often lead to inefficiencies and delays in responding to urgent global challenges. This bureaucratic inertia can hinder the organization's ability to adapt quickly to emerging crises or changing circumstances.

Furthermore, there are concerns about the transparency and accountability of UN agencies and programs, as well as allegations of corruption and mismanagement in some instances. These issues can undermine public trust in the organization and its ability to effectively deliver on its mandates.

Another significant criticism of the UN is its historical lack of inclusivity and representation, particularly in its founding structure. When the UN was established in 1945 in the aftermath of World War II, **no African country was invited to participate in the discussions and negotiations that shaped its setup,** despite the significant contributions and sacrifices made by **millions of Africans who fought for the Allied powers** during the war. This exclusion reflects a broader pattern of colonial-era power dynamics and Eurocentric perspectives that continue to influence global governance structures.

While the United Nations plays a vital role in promoting peace, security, and development worldwide, it faces inherent structural challenges that can impede its effectiveness. Addressing these issues requires a commitment to reforming and democratizing the organization to ensure greater inclusivity, transparency, and accountability in decision-making processes.

Let's add some examples to illustrate the problems with the UN structure:

1. **Imbalance of Power in the Security Council:** The veto power held by the five

permanent members of the Security Council has led to instances where critical actions, such as resolutions to address humanitarian crises or conflicts, have been blocked due to disagreements among these major powers. For example, Russia and China have used their veto power to block resolutions on Syria, resulting in prolonged suffering and a lack of meaningful international intervention.

2. **Disparities in General Assembly Representation:** While the General Assembly theoretically provides each member state with equal representation, the influence of larger and more economically powerful countries can overshadow that of smaller nations. For instance, decisions on budget allocations and key resolutions may be dominated by the interests of a few powerful states, marginalizing the voices of smaller countries.

3. **Bureaucratic Inefficiencies:** The UN's bureaucratic structure can lead to inefficiencies and delays in decision-making, particularly in responding to urgent crises. For example, during the 2014 Ebola outbreak in West Africa, bureaucratic hurdles and delays in mobilizing resources hindered the UN's initial response efforts, exacerbating the spread of the disease and its impact on affected populations.

4. **Transparency and Accountability Concerns:** There have been instances of

corruption and mismanagement within UN agencies and programs, raising concerns about transparency and accountability. For example, allegations of fraud and embezzlement within the Oil-for-Food program in Iraq in the early 2000s tarnished the reputation of the UN and highlighted weaknesses in oversight and accountability mechanisms.

5. **Historical Lack of Inclusivity:** The exclusion of African countries from the discussions and negotiations that shaped the UN's founding structure is a stark example of its historical lack of inclusivity. Despite the significant contributions of African soldiers and civilians to the Allied victory in World War II, their voices were not heard in the establishment of the post-war international order, reflecting enduring patterns of colonial-era power dynamics and Eurocentric perspectives.

These examples illustrate the structural challenges facing the United Nations and underscore the need for ongoing reform efforts to address issues of power imbalances, bureaucratic inefficiencies, and historical injustices.

In democracies, the principle of majority rule is often regarded as a cornerstone of governance, yet it can conceal underlying injustices when wielded unchecked. The notion of the "tyranny of the majority" emerges when the interests and preferences of the majority overpower and marginalize those of the minority, resulting in systemic oppression and discrimination. This imbalance challenges democracy's professed commitment to equality and inclusivity, revealing the fragility of individual rights and freedoms in the face of majority dominance.

One poignant example of the tyranny of the majority can be observed in the history of civil rights struggles. In the United States, for instance, the era of Jim Crow laws epitomized the exploitation of democratic processes to enforce racial segregation and disenfranchise African Americans. Despite being a minority population, African Americans faced institutionalized discrimination sanctioned by the majority through legislation and societal norms. The suppression of minority voting rights and the imposition of racially discriminatory policies illustrate how democratic structures can perpetuate injustice when wielded to serve the interests of the dominant group.

Similarly, LGBTQ+ rights have been a battleground where the tyranny of the majority has manifested in democratic societies. In many countries, the majority has historically wielded its influence to deny basic rights and protections to LGBTQ+ individuals, often citing popular sentiment or religious beliefs to justify discriminatory laws and policies. For example, laws criminalizing same-sex relationships or denying marriage equality have persisted in democratic nations, reflecting the enduring influence of majority prejudice and bias.

Furthermore, the plight of indigenous peoples serves as a stark reminder of how democratic systems can fail to protect minority rights. Across the globe, indigenous communities have faced dispossession of their lands, cultural erasure, and marginalization at the hands of majority-dominated governments. Despite international recognition of indigenous rights, democratic governments have often prioritized economic interests or development projects over the rights and sovereignty of indigenous peoples, perpetuating cycles of injustice and inequality.

Here are a few examples on the plight of indigenous peoples across different countries:

Australia: In Australia, Aboriginal and Torres Strait Islander peoples have endured centuries of dispossession, discrimination, and cultural suppression. The forced removal of Indigenous children from their families under government assimilation policies, known as the Stolen Generations, is a dark chapter in Australian history. Despite legal recognition of Indigenous land rights and the establishment of native title legislation, Indigenous communities continue to face challenges in reclaiming and protecting their traditional lands from development projects and resource extraction.

New Zealand: The Treaty of Waitangi, signed between the British Crown and Māori chiefs in 1840, promised to protect Māori rights to land and resources. However, subsequent land confiscations, breaches of the treaty, and cultural assimilation policies have marginalized Māori communities and eroded their sovereignty. Despite efforts to address historical grievances through treaty settlements and the establishment of Māori representation in parliament, disparities in health, education, and socioeconomic outcomes persist.

USA: Indigenous peoples in the United States, including Native American tribes and Alaska Natives, have faced similar challenges to their land, sovereignty, and cultural identity. The legacy of forced removal, broken treaties, and government assimilation policies, such as the Indian Removal Act and the Indian Boarding School system, has resulted in intergenerational trauma and loss of traditional lands. Despite legal recognition of tribal sovereignty and self-determination rights, Indigenous communities continue to grapple with issues such as poverty, inadequate healthcare, and environmental degradation on tribal lands.

Canada: Indigenous peoples in Canada, including First Nations, Métis, and Inuit communities, have endured a legacy of colonialism, dispossession, and systemic discrimination. The Indian Act, enacted in 1876, imposed paternalistic policies aimed at assimilating Indigenous peoples into Euro-Canadian society and restricting their rights to land, culture, and self-governance. Despite efforts to reconcile with Indigenous peoples through initiatives such as the Truth and Reconciliation Commission and land claim settlements, disparities in education, healthcare, and social services persist.

China: In China, ethnic minority groups, including Tibetans, Uighurs, and Mongolians, have faced state-sponsored assimilation policies and cultural suppression. The Chinese government's control over autonomous regions such as Tibet and Xinjiang has led to allegations of human rights abuses, including forced labor, mass surveillance, and religious persecution. Despite constitutional guarantees of autonomy and cultural rights for ethnic minorities, the Chinese Communist Party's prioritization of political stability and economic development has marginalized indigenous communities and eroded their cultural identity.

England: In England, the historical colonization of indigenous peoples in territories such as Australia, New Zealand, and North America exemplifies the tyranny of the majority's oppression. British colonial policies, including land seizures, forced resettlement, and cultural assimilation, resulted in the dispossession and marginalization of indigenous communities worldwide. Despite decolonization efforts and acknowledgment of historical injustices, the legacy of British imperialism continues to impact indigenous peoples' lives and rights.

Ireland: The history of British colonization and the Anglo-Irish conflict in Ireland highlight the plight of indigenous peoples facing oppression from a dominant majority. Centuries of British rule, including land confiscations, religious discrimination, and cultural suppression, led to the marginalization and disenfranchisement of the Irish population. Despite Ireland's independence, sectarian tensions and discrimination against Irish Travellers and other marginalized groups persist, highlighting ongoing challenges in achieving equality and justice for indigenous peoples.

India: India's diverse indigenous communities, often referred to as Scheduled Tribes or Adivasis, have faced marginalization and displacement due to development projects, resource extraction, and land conflicts. Government policies aimed at economic growth and modernization have often disregarded indigenous land rights and cultural traditions, leading to conflicts over land ownership and environmental degradation. Despite legal protections and affirmative action measures, indigenous communities continue to face challenges in asserting their rights and preserving their cultural heritage.

Europe: Indigenous peoples in Europe, including the Sami in Scandinavia and the

Basques in Spain, have struggled to maintain their cultural identity and land rights in the face of majority dominance. Historical assimilation policies, such as forced relocation and cultural suppression, have threatened the survival of indigenous languages, traditions, and ways of life. Despite international recognition of indigenous rights and efforts to promote cultural diversity, challenges persist in achieving full recognition and respect for indigenous peoples' rights within European societies.

Even in contemporary democratic societies, the tyranny of the majority continues to manifest in various forms, from restrictive immigration policies that target minority groups to discriminatory practices in housing, employment, and education. These examples underscore the urgent need for mechanisms to safeguard minority rights and ensure that democratic processes are truly inclusive and equitable for all members of society. Without such safeguards, democracy risks becoming a tool for oppression rather than a vehicle for justice and progress.

True governance should transcend the whims of the majority and embrace the collective will of all citizens. The essence of democracy lies not in the rule of the majority, but in the protection of minority rights and the representation of diverse interests. Moreover, the intrusion of business interests into the political sphere further distorts this ideal, turning governance into a transactional affair driven by profit motives rather than public welfare.

True governance should indeed transcend the fleeting preferences of the majority and instead uphold the rights and interests of all citizens, including minority groups.

In **Australia**, for instance, embracing true governance would entail honoring the land rights and cultural heritage of Indigenous peoples, ensuring their voices are heard and respected in decision-making processes related to land use and resource management. This could involve establishing mechanisms for meaningful consultation and collaboration between Indigenous communities and government agencies, as well as implementing policies that prioritize Indigenous self-determination and sustainable development.

Similarly, in **New Zealand**, true governance would involve upholding the principles of the Treaty of Waitangi and actively addressing historical injustices and disparities faced by Māori communities. This could include implementing equitable policies in areas such as education, healthcare, and economic development, as well as providing adequate resources and support for Māori-led initiatives aimed at revitalizing language and culture. Additionally, fostering genuine partnerships between the government and Māori authorities could help ensure that decisions affecting Māori interests are made collaboratively and with mutual respect.

In the **United States**, true governance would require a commitment to dismantling systemic racism and addressing the legacies of colonialism and oppression faced by Indigenous peoples and other marginalized communities. This could involve implementing reforms to promote racial equity in areas such as criminal justice, housing, and healthcare, as well as supporting initiatives to empower Indigenous nations and promote cultural revitalization. Furthermore, reducing the influence of corporate interests in politics and promoting transparency and accountability in government decision-making processes would be essential to ensuring that governance serves the public interest rather than corporate profit.

In **Canada**, true governance would involve honoring the spirit and intent of treaties and reconciliation agreements with Indigenous peoples, as well as implementing concrete measures to address ongoing injustices and inequalities. This could include providing adequate funding and resources for Indigenous-led initiatives in areas such as education, healthcare, and economic development, as well as supporting efforts to restore Indigenous land rights and promote self-governance. Additionally, fostering a culture of respect for Indigenous knowledge and perspectives within government institutions and society at large would be crucial to building trust and fostering meaningful dialogue and collaboration.

In **China**, true governance would entail respecting the rights and autonomy of ethnic minority groups, including Tibetans, Uighurs, and Mongolians, and addressing systemic discrimination and human rights abuses. This could involve repealing repressive policies such as mass surveillance and forced assimilation, as well as promoting dialogue and negotiation to address grievances and resolve conflicts peacefully. Additionally, promoting cultural diversity and inclusivity within Chinese society and institutions would be essential to fostering social harmony and stability.

In **England**, Ireland, India, and Europe, true governance would involve acknowledging and addressing historical injustices and inequalities faced by indigenous peoples and marginalized communities, as well as promoting inclusive policies and practices that respect diversity and protect human rights. This could include implementing affirmative action measures to promote equal opportunities and representation for minority groups, as well as investing in programs and initiatives aimed at addressing poverty, discrimination, and social exclusion. Furthermore, fostering a culture of accountability and transparency in government institutions and promoting civic engagement and participation would be essential to ensuring that governance serves the interests of all citizens and promotes the common good.

In the upcoming chapters, we delve into practical strategies for achieving a governance model that truly reflects the collective will of all citizens, both within individual countries and on a global scale. Central to this vision is the concept of "Peopleize," which advocates for the active participation of each person in decision-making processes, fostering inclusivity, equity, and accountability. By prioritizing the voices and needs of everyday people over the influence of special interests, such as corporate lobbyists, we can shift the focus of governance towards policies that prioritize the well-being of all individuals and promote a more sustainable, equal, and safe community for every person.

At the National Level:

1. **Citizen Assemblies:** Implementing citizen assemblies or deliberative democracy mechanisms allows for diverse voices to be heard in policymaking. Randomly selected citizens represent the population and deliberate on issues, ensuring a more inclusive and representative decision-making process.

2. **Decentralized Governance:** Devolving power to local communities empowers individuals to participate directly in decisions that affect their lives. By decentralizing

governance structures, we enable grassroots initiatives and localized solutions that are responsive to the unique needs and contexts of different regions.

3. **Transparency and Accountability:** Strengthening transparency measures and accountability mechanisms within government institutions enhances public trust and fosters greater citizen engagement. Open access to information, robust oversight mechanisms, and measures to prevent corruption are essential for ensuring that government actions align with the interests of the people.

At the Global Level:

1. **International Cooperation:** Emphasizing collaboration and cooperation among nations is crucial for addressing global challenges such as climate change, poverty, and public health crises. Multilateral agreements and frameworks facilitate joint action and solidarity across borders, amplifying the collective impact of individual countries.

2. **Global Citizens' Assembly:** Establishing a global citizens' assembly or forum provides a platform for people from around the world to participate in shaping international policies and agendas. By ensuring diverse representation and inclusivity, such a forum can promote global solidarity and address shared challenges through collective action.

3. **Democratic Reform of International Institutions:** Reforming international institutions, such as the United Nations and World Bank, to be more democratic and accountable to the people they serve is essential. This includes enhancing the representation of marginalized groups, increasing transparency in decision-making processes, and reducing the influence of powerful nations and corporate interests.

By embracing the principles of PEOPLEIZE and prioritizing the participation of every person, we can create governance structures that truly serve the common good. Removing the undue influence of business interests and prioritizing collaboration over partisan politics paves the way for a more just, equitable, and sustainable world for present and future generations.

Chapter ii

PEOPLEIZE Government by the People

In envisioning a more just and equitable future, it's imperative to reimagine the very essence of governance. The concept of PEOPLEIZE government proposes a radical departure from traditional paradigms, where power emanates not from the top down, but from the people up.

At its core, PEOPLEIZE government entails the active participation of all segments of society in the decision-making process. Rather than relegating governance to a select cadre of politicians, removing power distributed and replacing it with a random selection of people that receive the same pay and are randomly selected to local, regional and national government each year from the countries diverse array of people, workers' unions, industry union, and the general populace.

By divorcing politics from business interests, we pave the way for a more transparent and accountable form of governance. Instead of serving the narrow agendas of corporations or elite factions, government becomes a vehicle for collective collaboration aimed at fostering the common good.

Central to the concept of PEOPLEIZE government is the recognition that true progress cannot be achieved through narrow nationalistic or monetary aims. Instead, governance must transcend borders and prioritize the holistic well-being of humanity and the planet.

By embracing diversity, equity, and inclusivity, we can forge a path towards a more just and sustainable future. Through the collaborative efforts of all segments of society, we can build a world where governance truly reflects the will of the people and serves the interests of the collective whole.

How would the PEOPLEIZE Government by the people work?

In each country there are various industries, organizations and employee unions. These chapters or unions play pivotal roles in shaping societal dynamics. Industries such as agriculture, manufacturing, technology, healthcare, education, transportation, and finance form the backbone of economic activity. Additionally, non-profit organizations, advocacy groups, trade unions, and professional associations contribute to the socio-political landscape, representing the interests of diverse sectors of society.

Estimated Number of Industries, Employee Unions, Organizations, and NGOs currently registered in South Africa, Thailand, Germany and Tanzania:

Category	Germany	Thailand	Tanzania	South Africa
Industries	1,000	500	300	700
Employee Unions	500	300	200	400
Organizations	10,000	8,000	5,000	20,000

Some industries, unions, and organizations will represent overlapping areas of interest, resulting in a lower total number of distinct entities, ensuring that there is no monopoly or dominance from any specific industries, unions, or organizations.

Under the PEOPLEIZE framework, each of these industries, organizations, and unions establishes a committee comprised of 12 to 30 randomly selected members from the employees annually. These committees serve as microcosms of their respective sectors, ensuring that a broad spectrum of voices is represented. Through this random selection process, the committees reflect the diversity and dynamism of their constituents, fostering inclusivity and equitable representation of each organization, union or industry.

During the Equinox (Vernal), the initial selection process occurs across all cities, wherein committees comprised of 12 to 30 individuals representing various fields, industries, unions, and organizations are formed for their respective fields, industries, unions and organization. For example in all cities around the world committees are established to represent the interests of sectors such as education, healthcare, manufacturing, construction worker, agriculture, and more. These committees serve as platforms for local employees and citizens to voice their concerns and priorities in their respective fields, industries, unions and organization. For instance, in Dar es Salaam, a committee consisting of 12 to 30 teachers create the local teachers union for the city to represent educational interests, additional in Dar es Salaam, another committee representing healthcare workers would be formed. These representatives are chosen to advocate for their specific sectors and bring forth their expertise and perspectives to be considered in city, state and national decision-making processes. Creating a collaboration opportunity for the citizens and sustainability of their communities.

Following their representation of various fields and industries for 6 months at the Equinox (Autumnal), a new phase of the PEOPLEIZE Government process begins. From the pool of committee members, individuals are randomly selected to serve as representatives at the city, state and national government levels. This random selection ensures fairness and prevents any undue influence or bias in the selection process.

Once chosen, these individuals assume their roles as government representatives, tasked with advocating for the interests of their respective fields, organization and unions within the governmental sphere. Their direct involvement in governance fosters collaboration and ensures that decisions are made with the input and participation of all stakeholders. This collaborative approach embodies the spirit of WOBUNTU the African philosophy that emphasizes the interconnectedness of people and the truth that "I am, because we are."

Moreover, since everyone receives the same salary (50,000) regardless of their role in government or their profession, there is no need for monetary incentives. This community collaboration is driven by a shared commitment to the common good rather than individual gain. By removing financial disparities and emphasizing collective well-being, the system encourages cooperation and solidarity among all members of society.

The goal at each PEOPLEIZE governmental level is to ensure that we all collaborate and create an equal, sustainable society for all people, not just within our field, industry, organization, or union. Understanding that the artificial paper monetary system we use, is meant to support, not control, our government and Earth's sustainability.

This rotational system not only promotes inclusivity and equal participation but also ensures a continuous influx of fresh perspectives and ideas into the governance process. By providing everyone with the opportunity to serve and be part of representing their fields and communities, the system fosters a sense of civic engagement and empowers individuals to actively contribute to the betterment of society.

To maintain the integrity of the random selection process and prevent any potential corruption or undue influence, a robust system is implemented at all levels of government. At the onset of each government representative's session, new employees are hired for the positions that are vacate from the previous government representative. These new employees undergo a transparent application process, ensuring equal opportunity for all interested candidates.

During the hiring process, multiple rounds of evaluation are conducted, ultimately leading to the selection of three final applicants for each position. These finalists are chosen through a combination of qualifications, experience, and suitability for the role. Importantly, the selection of these finalists is done randomly, further safeguarding against favoritism or bias.

Once the finalists are identified, the randomly selected government representative will then make the final hiring decision form the 3 finalist. Each new employee selected for a government position serves a one year period. This rotational model ensures that both the government representative and their office employees have equal opportunities to serve in government and contribute to the decision-making process. Both receive the same salary as every other person in the country and on earth (50,000) so there is no need for monetary greed.

Upon the completion of their government 1 year tenure, the government representative and employee will return back to their community and their original jobs. This cyclical arrangement ensures a seamless transition of responsibilities and allows for the ongoing rotation of individuals between government and their respective professions.

By upholding transparent hiring practices and ensuring random selection, this system maintains the integrity and fairness of government appointments while providing opportunities for broader participation and engagement in governance. It removes the idea of a political career and big business lobbying.

Outline of Government by The People:

➢ **Annual Formation of Committees:** At the Equinox (Vernal), committees representing various fields, industries, unions, and organizations are established in all cities. These committees consist of 12 to 30 randomly selected members who serve for one year for each of the various fields, industries, unions and organizations.

- **Representation city, state and national Government at the Equinox Autumnal:** After serving their respective sectors for 6 months, members of the committees become eligible for selection as representatives at the city, state, or national government levels. This selection occurs at the Equinox Autumnal, ensuring fairness and preventing bias.

- **Random Selection of Government Representatives:** From the pool of committee members, individuals are randomly chosen to serve as government representatives. These representatives advocate for the interests of their sectors within the governmental sphere for the remainder of the year.

- **Equal Salaries and Community Collaboration:** Every person on earth receives the same salary for their job. In addition throughout their tenure in government, representatives receive the same salary as every other individual in the country, emphasizing community collaboration over monetary gain.

- **Continuous Influx of Fresh Perspectives:** The rotational system ensures a continuous influx of fresh perspectives into the governance process. Upon completion of their tenure, government representatives and their replacements return to their original roles within their communities and professions.

▷ **Transparent Hiring Practices:** To maintain the integrity of the process, new employees are hired each year for the positions vacated by government representatives. This hiring process includes multiple rounds of evaluation, culminating in the random selection of three final applicants for each position.

▷ **Seamless Transition and Ongoing Rotation:** Upon the completion of their government tenure, both the government representatives and their replacements seamlessly transition back to their original roles within their communities and professions. This cyclical arrangement allows for the ongoing rotation of individuals between government and their respective sectors.

The PEOPLEIZE Government by the people model offers several positive aspects:

▷ **Inclusive Representation:** By establishing committees comprising randomly selected members from various sectors, industries, organizations, and unions, the model ensures that a diverse range of voices and perspectives are represented in governance. This inclusivity fosters a more representative and equitable decision-making process that takes into account the needs and priorities of different segments of society.

- ▷ **Promotion of Civic Engagement:** The model encourages active participation in governance by providing opportunities for individuals to serve as government representatives at different levels. This fosters a sense of civic engagement and empowers individuals to play an active role in shaping the policies and decisions that affect their communities.

- ▷ **Prevention of Corruption and Bias:** Through transparent hiring practices and random selection processes, the model safeguards against favoritism, corruption, and undue influence in government appointments. By ensuring equal opportunity for all interested candidates and minimizing the potential for bias, the model upholds the integrity and fairness of government representation.

- ▷ **Community Collaboration:** The emphasis on equal salaries for all individuals, regardless of their role in government or profession, promotes a sense of community collaboration and collective well-being over individual gain. This fosters cooperation and solidarity among members of society, driving governance decisions that prioritize the common good.

- ▷ **Continuous Renewal of Perspectives:** The rotational system ensures a continuous influx of fresh perspectives and ideas into the governance process. By periodically rotating government representatives and employees between government and their respective sectors, the model promotes innovation, adaptability, and responsiveness to evolving societal needs and challenges.

> **Seamless Transition and Stability:** The cyclical arrangement of transitioning government representatives back to their original roles within their communities and professions ensures stability and continuity in governance. This seamless transition allows for the ongoing rotation of individuals between government and their respective sectors, maintaining the balance between public service and professional responsibilities.

The PEOPLEIZE Government by the people model offers a positive framework for fostering inclusive, transparent, and participatory governance that prioritizes the interests of all members of society. By addressing the challenges of traditional governance systems and promoting collaboration, accountability, and civic engagement, the model holds the potential to create more responsive and effective governance structures in diverse contexts.

Here are some Challenges and Solutions:

Challenge: Resistance to Change	Solution: Building Awareness and Consensus
Overcoming entrenched power structures and traditional dynamics within society may pose significant hurdles to the adoption of the PEOPLEIZE model.	Engage in dialogue with political elites, bureaucrats, and the public to address concerns and garner support for the model. - Conduct advocacy campaigns showcasing the benefits of the PEOPLEIZE model and its potential to enhance inclusivity and participation in governance.
Challenge: Complexity of Implementation	**Solution: Capacity Building and Training**
Establishing and managing the administrative infrastructure required for the PEOPLEIZE model may be complex and resource-intensive.	Offer training programs on random selection processes, transparent hiring practices, and administrative management to government officials and administrators. - Develop resources and support systems to facilitate efficient implementation and management of the PEOPLEIZE framework at all levels of government.
Challenge: Ensuring Representation	**Solution: Enhancing Representation**
Ensuring diverse representation within the committees and government representatives is crucial for the legitimacy and effectiveness of the PEOPLEIZE model.	Implement targeted outreach programs to marginalized communities to encourage their participation in the selection process. - Consider the adoption of quota systems or affirmative action policies within the selection process to address historical inequalities and biases.
Challenge: Maintaining Accountability	**Solution: Establishing Robust Accountability Mechanisms**

With frequent turnover of government representatives, ensuring accountability and continuity in governance becomes essential.	Institute regular performance evaluations for government representatives to assess their effectiveness and adherence to ethical standards. - Establish independent oversight bodies tasked with monitoring the actions and decisions of government representatives to ensure transparency and integrity in governance.
Challenge: Managing Economic Impact	**Solution: Economic Impact Assessment**
Implementing a standardized salary for all individuals, regardless of their role in government or profession, may have significant economic implications.	Conduct a comprehensive economic impact assessment to evaluate the potential effects of the PEOPLEIZE model on fiscal sustainability, income distribution, and overall economic well-being. - Explore strategies for balancing equitable compensation with fiscal responsibility to mitigate adverse economic consequences.
Challenge: Cultural and Contextual Adaptation	**Solution: Contextual Adaptation**
Adapting the PEOPLEIZE model to suit the cultural, social, and political contexts of each country is essential for its successful implementation.	Consult with local stakeholders to understand the unique needs and circumstances of each community and tailor the model accordingly. - Incorporate feedback from diverse communities throughout the design and implementation process to ensure relevance and effectiveness.
Challenge: Iterative Approach and Learning	**Solution: Embracing an Iterative Approach**

Recognizing that no governance model is perfect, embracing an iterative approach to implementation allows for continuous learning and improvement.	Regularly evaluate the implementation of the PEOPLEIZE model, learn from both successes and challenges encountered, and be open to making adjustments based on feedback and experience. - Foster a culture of innovation and adaptation within the governance system to ensure its ongoing relevance and effectiveness in meeting the evolving needs of society.

In addition to implementing the PEOPLEIZE model at the local, state, and national levels, a similar approach is adopted for the United Nations (UN) and global governance. At the conclusion of their terms serving in various capacities within city, state, and national governments, individuals from each country are randomly selected to represent their respective countries at the global level. This selection process ensures that a diverse array of voices and perspectives from different countries are represented on the global stage.

Each country nominates a total of 15 individuals through this random selection process, reflecting a cross-section of society and expertise within the nation. These representatives serve as delegates to various international forums, including the United Nations General Assembly, specialized agencies, and other global decision-making bodies. Their role is to advocate for the interests of their country while also collaborating with representatives from other nations to address pressing global challenges and advance common goals.

The bedrock of this global governance framework is a focus on equality for all, recognizing that the current monetary system is artificially created by humans. It emphasizes that the monetary system should be used to facilitate equality and not greed. This perspective drives efforts to remove the need for inheritance and interest rates, remove inflation (which is human made), and remove other unjust practices designed to favor specific groups and countries.

The selection of representatives for global governance follows similar principles of transparency, inclusivity, and equitable participation as observed at the local and national levels. By involving individuals chosen through random selection rather than appointment or election, the global governance framework aims to mitigate biases, promote diversity, and ensure that the voices of ordinary citizens are heard and considered in shaping global policies and initiatives.

Further details regarding the selection process, roles, and responsibilities of global representatives will be elaborated upon in upcoming publications, providing insight into how the PEOPLEIZE model extends to the realm of international governance and contributes to fostering a more inclusive and participatory global community.

Chapter iii

The Day After Gaza Genocide

In the aftermath of World War I and World War II, post-conflict reconstruction efforts often repeated mistakes, perpetuating inequality and marginalization. By examining these historical periods, we highlight the need to learn from past errors to avoid neo-colonialism. The PEOPLEIZE government concept, emphasizing empowerment and inclusion, offers a framework for building a more equitable society. Through prioritizing empowerment, addressing inequalities, promoting collaboration, and respecting sovereignty, we can chart a path towards a future free from the shadows of colonialism and conflict.

Learning from History: Avoiding Neo-Colonialism in Post-Conflict Reconstruction

After both World War I and World War II, the world witnessed significant efforts to reshape the global order. However, in many cases, the mistakes of the past were repeated, resulting in the imposition of new structures that marginalized certain populations and perpetuated systems of inequality. By examining these historical periods, we can glean valuable lessons for creating a more inclusive society in the aftermath of conflicts.

World War I: The Seeds of Discontent

Following World War I, the Treaty of Versailles imposed punitive measures on Germany and redrew borders across Europe and the Middle East. While the treaty aimed to maintain peace, its terms sowed seeds of resentment and economic instability, contributing to the rise of fascism and ultimately World War II. The reordering of territories and mandates in the Middle East by colonial powers disregarded the aspirations of local populations, setting the stage for decades of conflict and exploitation.

World War II: Missed Opportunities for Inclusion

In the aftermath of World War II, the victorious powers established the United Nations and implemented various initiatives to rebuild war-torn societies and prevent future conflicts. However, the division of the world into spheres of influence, such as the Cold War division of Europe and proxy conflicts in Asia and Africa, perpetuated colonial structures under new guises. The process of decolonization, while offering independence to some nations, often left them economically dependent and vulnerable to exploitation by former colonial powers or emerging superpowers.

Lessons Learned for Building an Inclusive Society

1. **Empowerment Over Imposition:** Rather than imposing solutions from above, post-conflict reconstruction efforts must prioritize empowering local communities and respecting their agency. True stability and prosperity can only be achieved when the voices and needs of all stakeholders are taken into account.

2. **Addressing Structural Inequalities:** Efforts to rebuild societies must address the root causes of conflict, including structural inequalities based on race, ethnicity, and economic disparity. This requires comprehensive reforms in governance, economic systems, and social policies to ensure equal opportunities for all citizens.

3. **Promoting Genuine Collaboration:** Building a more inclusive society necessitates genuine collaboration among nations, guided by principles of mutual respect, equality, and solidarity. International cooperation should aim to uplift marginalized communities and promote sustainable development, rather than perpetuating systems of exploitation and dominance.

4. **Respecting Sovereignty and Self-Determination:** Respecting the sovereignty and self-determination of nations is essential in preventing the recurrence of neo-colonial

practices. International interventions should be guided by principles of consent and support for locally-led initiatives, rather than imposing external agendas.

The mistakes made in the aftermath of World War I and World War II underscore the importance of learning from history to create a more inclusive and equitable society. By prioritizing empowerment, addressing structural inequalities, promoting collaboration, and respecting sovereignty, we can chart a path towards a future free from the shadows of colonialism and conflict.

The Day After Gaza Genocide

Initiating the Transition to a PEOPLEIZE Government Model.

We The People:

Initiating the transition towards a PEOPLEIZE governance model necessitates proactive engagement with the populace. This entails launching comprehensive public awareness campaigns, organizing town hall meetings, and facilitating interactive forums to enlighten citizens about the fundamental principles and advantages of PEOPLEIZE governance. A pivotal initial step involves assisting in the establishment of local community committees that comprise a diverse representation including local businesses, trade unions, grassroots organizations, and community members. These committees serve as platforms for fostering collaboration within the local communities, ensuring that the transition to PEOPLEIZE governance is rooted in grassroots involvement and collective decision-making. By empowering communities to take ownership of the governance process, we lay the groundwork for a more inclusive and participatory society where the voices of all citizens are heard and valued.

Educating the Community:

Launching widespread educational initiatives is essential to ensure that citizens are well-informed about the concept of PEOPLEIZE governance, its underlying principles, and its departure from traditional governance models. This educational effort spans various channels, including social media campaigns, public seminars, educational workshops, and community outreach programs. For instance, local community centers could serve as hubs for hosting workshops that delve into the core tenets of PEOPLEIZE governance, elucidating how individuals can actively engage and contribute to the process.

Moreover, creating local unions or chapters for diverse sectors such as farmers, teachers, street vendors, and others is crucial for fostering understanding and empowerment among communities. These unions provide platforms for members to comprehend their collective influence and role in shaping governance through collaboration rather than oppression. By emphasizing the collective power of the people over that of big businesses, these initiatives instill a sense of agency and unity among citizens. Through mutual support and collaboration, communities can effect transformative change, ushering in a society founded on principles of equality and justice.

Fostering Civic Participation:

Fostering civic participation entails actively engaging and involving all segments of society by creating inclusive platforms for dialogue, feedback, and collaboration. This can be achieved through the establishment of various mechanisms such as citizen forums, online discussion boards, and participatory decision-making processes that enable individuals to contribute their ideas, concerns, and aspirations for the future of governance.

For instance, setting up online platforms where citizens can submit policy suggestions and vote on issues important to them facilitates direct engagement and ensures that the voices of the people are heard in decision-making processes. Additionally, encouraging the newly formed worker chapters or unions to run for local governmental offices using the PEOPLEIZE model amplifies local voices at the government level and kickstarts the transformation process.

It's important to recognize that unity among the people is paramount in the face of attempts by politicians and big businesses to divide and conquer. By educating each other about the power of unity and the shared vision of creating an equal, violence-free, and sustainable Earth for all, we can counteract these divisive forces. Together, we the people hold the power to shape our collective future and create a society that prioritizes the well-being of all its members, not just a privileged few.

Empowering PEOPLEIZE Movements:

Empowering people at all levels to align closely with the principles of the PEOPLEIZE governance model, which emphasizes inclusivity, transparency, and accountability in governance. By supporting local movements and civil society organizations that champion these principles, we can catalyze positive change from the ground up.

Collaborating with community leaders, activists, and advocates is key to mobilizing support and building momentum for the adoption of PEOPLEIZE governance at various levels – local, regional, and national. This collaboration involves providing resources and training to local activists who are at the forefront of promoting PEOPLEIZE governance in their communities.

For example, local organizations advocating for environmental sustainability may receive support in organizing educational workshops on PEOPLEIZE governance principles and their relevance to environmental policy. Similarly, civil society groups focusing on social justice issues could benefit from training sessions on how to effectively engage with local government officials and mobilize community members to demand accountability and transparency in decision-making processes. By connecting all people we make our voices louder and stronger.

Furthermore, bringing together these diverse groups, environmental activists, social justice advocates, workers' unions, and community organizations, serves to strengthen the collective voice of grassroots movements. By facilitating collaboration and dialogue among these groups, we emphasize the common goal of creating a future of equality for all. Together, we realize that our voices are stronger when united, and that we are all working towards the same vision of a more equitable and sustainable society.

Mobilizing People For Action:

Initiating coordinated mass actions on each Equinox Vernal & Autumnal (representing the earth day of equality) by encouraging people to take a day off from work to demonstrate their support for PEOPLEIZE governance is a pivotal step towards manifesting the collective will of humanity for a more equitable world. By selecting these days of balance, when light and darkness are equal, we symbolize our commitment to achieving harmony and equality in governance.

Uniting various organizations and unions representing diverse causes and interests, we orchestrate peaceful sit-ins and demonstrations on the vernal and autumnal equinoxes. These gatherings serve as powerful expressions of solidarity and determination, showcasing our shared vision of a world governed by the people, for the people.

By mobilizing individuals from all walks of life, environmental activists, workers' unions, social justice advocates, and community organizations, we amplify the collective voice of "We the People." Together, we stand as a formidable force, demonstrating to governments worldwide that 7.9 billion individuals are united in their demand for governance that prioritizes the needs and aspirations of all citizens, not just a select few.

These mass actions serve as a resounding declaration that the era of governance dominated by a handful of leaders and big businesses is over. Instead, we advocate for a governance model where the voices of every individual are heard and valued, where freedom and equality are upheld regardless of nationality, personality, or birthright.

Through organizing rallies, marches, and other public events, we raise awareness and galvanize support for PEOPLEIZE governance. These actions not only demand attention from policymakers but also inspire grassroots movements worldwide to join the cause. Ultimately, these coordinated efforts on the equinoxes lay the foundation for a future where every person can live in a world that stands for freedom, equality, and justice.

How Organizations, NGOs, and Companies Can Lead:

In addition to engaging the general populace, mobilizing support from various organizations is essential for the successful implementation of a PEOPLEIZE governance model. As entities vested in social responsibility and ethical governance, organizations, NGOs, and companies play a crucial role in driving positive change.

They should foster collaborative partnerships, not only locally but also regionally, nationally, and globally, amplifying advocacy efforts for inclusive and transparent governance structures. Encouraging companies to integrate PEOPLEIZE principles into their corporate social responsibility initiatives and advocating for policy reform at multiple levels further strengthens the collective voice for change. Investing in civic education, connecting communities, and sharing best practices contribute to fostering a culture of active citizenship and democratic participation across different regions and countries.

By leading by example and demonstrating commitment to ethical governance practices, organizations, NGOs, and companies inspire others to follow suit and contribute to building a more just and equitable society on a global scale. Through these collaborative efforts that unite individual groups into one voice, meaningful change towards a PEOPLEIZE governance model that truly serves the interests of "We the People" can be realized.

Businesses and Corporations:

Engaging with businesses and corporations is crucial to garner their support for PEOPLEIZE governance and demonstrate how it aligns with principles of corporate social responsibility, sustainability, and ethical business practices. Encouraging businesses to adopt inclusive decision-making processes and transparent governance structures within their organizations is essential for fostering a culture of accountability and fairness. Furthermore, promoting equality in salary across country boundaries and within their own company structures ensures parity between employees, investors, and CEOs, fostering a sense of equity and shared prosperity. Additionally, advocating for equal profit-sharing among all employees further reinforces the principles of inclusivity and fairness, ensuring that the benefits of economic success are distributed equitably among all stakeholders. By championing these values and practices, businesses and corporations can not only contribute to building a more just and equitable society but also enhance their own long-term sustainability and reputation as responsible corporate citizens.

Moreover, addressing disparities in payment to influencers based on their geographic location, despite charging the same cost for advertisements, is paramount. For instance, online media companies often pay different amounts to influencers depending on their geographical location, yet they charge the same amount for advertisements. This discrepancy undermines the principles of equality and fairness, and it highlights the need for businesses to ensure equal compensation for equal work, regardless of geographic location. Aligning payment structures with the principles of PEOPLEIZE governance fosters a more equitable and transparent business environment, where all individuals are valued and compensated fairly for their contributions.

Non-Profit Organizations and Advocacy Groups:

Collaborating with non-profit organizations, advocacy groups, and civil society organizations is instrumental in amplifying the voices of marginalized communities, promoting social justice, and advocating for the adoption of PEOPLEIZE governance policies and reforms. While these groups may represent diverse interests and communities, they share a common goal of creating a more inclusive, equitable, and sustainable society. By uniting their voices and leveraging their collective expertise, networks, and resources, they can mobilize grassroots support and drive meaningful change. Furthermore, by using the equinox as a day of equality and unity, these organizations can send a powerful message to politicians and governments about the people's desire to live in a world characterized by equality, peace, and sustainability. Through coordinated action and solidarity, non-profit organizations and advocacy groups can demonstrate the strength of their shared vision and advocate for policies that prioritize the well-being of all individuals and communities

Educational Institutions and Research Centers:

In a concerted effort to advance the principles of PEOPLEIZE governance, educational institutions, research centers, and academic networks are pivotal partners. Collaborating with Non-Profit Organizations and Advocacy Groups, these institutions can conduct research, develop educational materials, and train future leaders and policymakers in the principles and practices of PEOPLEIZE governance. By leveraging their academic expertise and resources, they can contribute valuable insights into the challenges and opportunities of implementing inclusive and transparent governance models. Moreover, integrating PEOPLEIZE concepts into school curricula, university programs, and professional training courses becomes imperative. This integration ensures that future generations are equipped with the knowledge and skills necessary to actively engage in civic affairs and promote participatory governance. Businesses and Corporations can also play a role by supporting educational initiatives and providing resources to facilitate this integration. Additionally, Mobilizing People For Action becomes central in this context.

By organizing awareness campaigns, workshops, and events within educational institutions, the broader community can be mobilized to advocate for PEOPLEIZE governance. Furthermore, by using the equinox as a day of equality and unity, educational institutions can join Non-Profit Organizations, Advocacy Groups, Businesses, and Corporations in demonstrating widespread support for equitable and participatory governance. Through these collaborative efforts, educational institutions and research centers become key drivers of change, fostering a culture of civic engagement and laying the groundwork for a more just and inclusive society.

How Government Can Change Peacefully:

Collaborating with governments at all levels is crucial for laying the groundwork for the transition to a PEOPLEIZE governance model. This involves engaging with policymakers to raise awareness about the principles and benefits of PEOPLEIZE government. By fostering dialogue and cooperation between government officials and civil society organizations, we can create pathways for policy reforms that prioritize inclusivity, transparency, and accountability.

Governments can play a central role in implementing PEOPLEIZE concepts by enacting legislation that promotes citizen participation in decision-making processes and ensures equal representation for all members of society. Additionally, establishing mechanisms for regular consultation and feedback between government agencies and the public can help build trust and confidence in the governance system. Furthermore, integrating PEOPLEIZE principles into government policies and programs, such as budget allocations and resource distribution, can ensure that the needs and priorities of all citizens are adequately addressed.

By working collaboratively with governments, we can create an enabling environment for the transition to a PEOPLEIZE governance model, where the voices of all individuals are heard and valued in shaping the future of society.

Building Political Will:

Engaging with elected officials, policymakers, and government agencies is crucial for building political will and consensus around the adoption of PEOPLEIZE governance principles. By advocating for the integration of PEOPLEIZE principles into government structures, we aim to transform governance systems to be more inclusive, transparent, and accountable. Highlighting the potential benefits of PEOPLEIZE governance, such as promoting democracy, enhancing transparency, and fostering citizen trust in government institutions, can help garner support from decision-makers.

By demonstrating how PEOPLEIZE governance empowers citizens and ensures their voices are heard in decision-making processes, we can inspire policymakers to champion reform initiatives. Additionally, showcasing successful case studies and examples of PEOPLEIZE governance implementations from around the world can provide tangible evidence of its effectiveness. Through sustained advocacy efforts and dialogue with government stakeholders, we can cultivate a shared understanding of the importance of PEOPLEIZE principles in shaping the future of governance. This collaborative approach fosters a conducive environment for policymakers to embrace PEOPLEIZE governance and enact reforms that reflect the will and interests of the people they serve.

Pilot Projects and Demonstrations:

Advocating for the implementation of pilot projects and demonstrations of PEOPLEIZE governance principles is a pivotal step towards showcasing its feasibility and effectiveness in real-world settings. By partnering with local governments, NGOs, and community stakeholders, we can identify suitable cities, regions, or government agencies willing to participate in these initiatives. These pilot projects serve as living laboratories, allowing us to test and refine PEOPLEIZE governance practices in diverse socio-political contexts. Through careful planning and collaboration, we design tailored interventions that prioritize inclusivity, transparency, and citizen participation.

Moreover, these pilot projects provide an opportunity to collect valuable data, monitor outcomes, and evaluate the impact of PEOPLEIZE governance initiatives. By employing rigorous evaluation methodologies, we assess the effectiveness of various strategies and identify best practices that can be replicated elsewhere. This evidence-based approach not only informs future policy decisions but also provides insights into the scalability and sustainability of PEOPLEIZE governance models.

Furthermore, by actively involving local communities in the design and implementation of these initiatives, we foster ownership and buy-in, ensuring that PEOPLEIZE governance resonates with the needs and aspirations of the people it serves. Through participatory processes such as town hall meetings, community consultations, and citizen assemblies, we empower individuals to shape the direction of governance reform and hold decision-makers accountable.

Ultimately, these pilot projects and demonstrations serve as catalysts for broader systemic change, inspiring governments at all levels to embrace PEOPLEIZE governance principles. By showcasing tangible examples of its impact on governance outcomes and citizen engagement, we pave the way for a more inclusive, transparent, and accountable future for all.

Legislative Reforms and Policy Amendments:

Working collaboratively with lawmakers and policy experts, we aim to propose legislative reforms and policy amendments that institutionalize PEOPLEIZE governance principles within existing legal frameworks. This multifaceted approach entails revising electoral laws to enhance fairness and inclusivity in the electoral process, restructuring government institutions to promote transparency and accountability, and establishing robust mechanisms for citizen participation and oversight.

Through dialogue and consultation with stakeholders, including civil society organizations, academic institutions, and grassroots movements, we identify key areas for legislative intervention and policy reform. By harnessing the collective expertise and insights of these diverse voices, we craft comprehensive reform proposals that address systemic barriers to effective governance and promote the values of PEOPLEIZE governance.

Furthermore, fostering public awareness and engagement is paramount in driving legislative change. By actively engaging the people through public forums, town hall meetings, and online campaigns, we empower citizens to advocate for legislative reforms that reflect their interests and aspirations. Mobilizing organizational support from NGOs, advocacy groups, and businesses amplifies our advocacy efforts and strengthens our collective voice in the policymaking process.

By collaborating with governments at all levels, we can navigate the complexities of the legislative process and build consensus around PEOPLEIZE governance principles. Through constructive dialogue and negotiation, we seek to garner political support for our reform agenda and secure passage of legislative measures that advance the transition to a more inclusive, transparent, and participatory form of governance.

The transition to a PEOPLEIZE governance model signifies far more than a mere bureaucratic overhaul; it marks a profound redefinition of societal values and norms. This metamorphosis necessitates a direct confrontation with the entrenched systems of violence, power, and colonization that have historically dictated our world's trajectory. By drawing upon the invaluable lessons of history, we come to acknowledge the dire repercussions of these systems, galvanizing our collective resolve to manifest a future characterized by universal peace and equality.

In order to realize this vision, it demands a unified commitment from the 7.9 billion inhabitants of Earth to perceive one another as equals, transcending the colonial biases ingrained within us, whether based on religion, ethnicity, or geography. Crucially, we must dismantle the very structures that perpetuate inequality and exploitation, steadfastly rejecting the notion of viewing fellow human beings as mere instruments for amassing wealth or as inherently inferior due to circumstances of birth or geographic location.

Through active engagement with communities, mobilization of organizational support, and collaboration with governments, we can meticulously lay the groundwork for legislative reforms and policy amendments that enshrine the principles of PEOPLEIZE governance. This concerted effort paves the way for a governance system that is genuinely responsive, accountable, and inclusive. In fostering such a system, we cultivate a world wherein every individual is bestowed with dignity, opportunity, and respect, thus heralding a future where equality is not merely an aspiration, but a tangible reality.

Regardless of the form of government a country adopts, the essence of true governance lies in the empowerment and involvement of ordinary citizens in decision-making processes. A system where the final decision-making power is not vested in the hands of common everyday people remains inherently colonial, as it perpetuates a fear of the views or voices of the populace. This fear, rooted in the desire to maintain control over the people, undermines the principles of equality, freedom, and democracy.

Big business interests and career politicians often contribute to this dynamic, further entrenching systems of inequality and exploitation for their own gain. We, the people, aspire to live in a society where power is decentralized, where decisions are made collectively, and where every individual's voice is heard and valued. This requires transcending the constraints of a monetary system inherited from a colonial era, which was designed to control and manipulate societies.

Instead, should build a governance model that prioritizes the well-being and interests of all people, ensuring a future built on principles of equality, freedom, and dignity for every member of society. Moreover, governments should refrain from engaging in conflicts over limited resources or land on Earth. Efforts should be directed towards preserving and sustainably managing these resources for the benefit of all people on Earth.

The world's countries military forces should be united under a common goal of planetary defense, preparing for the possibility of external threats from space. By cooperating rather than fighting amongst ourselves, we can better ensure the safety and security of our planet and its inhabitants. This collective approach also aligns with the broader goal of fostering peace and cooperation among nations, transcending borders and divisions to create a more harmonious world for future generations.

MY HEARTFELT GRATITUDE

In the moments of reflection while composing these words for "Government By The People: Decolonizing Governmental System," my heart overflows with gratitude. This work, an exploration of collaborative governance, peaceful community-building, sustainability, and the pursuit of shared prosperity, has been a journey unlike any other. To each reader who has embarked on this odyssey alongside me, I extend my sincerest thanks.

To those who have dared to challenge the status quo, to dream boldly, and to envision a world where unity prevails, your unwavering commitment to this transformative vision has been the driving force behind "PEOPLEIZE: Decolonizing Governmental System." I am profoundly grateful for your courage and your determination to push the boundaries of what is achievable.

Producing a work of such magnitude is never a solitary endeavor. I am immensely thankful to the countless individuals who have contributed, in various capacities, to the realization of "PEOPLEIZE: Decolonizing Governmental System." Your insights, support, and shared passion have played pivotal roles in bringing this vision to fruition.

To the trailblazers who advocate for the transformative potential of collaboration, to those who champion equality, justice, and understanding, and to every proponent of a more equitable world, this book stands as a testament to our collective aspirations. May the ideas conveyed within its pages spark dialogue, spur action, and instigate positive change in our communities and beyond.

To all who steadfastly believe in a future where peace, equality, harmony, and prosperity are shared by all, I express my deepest gratitude. "PEOPLEIZE: Decolonizing Governmental System" transcends mere literature; it serves as a guiding light towards a brighter tomorrow. Thank you for accompanying me on this remarkable journey.

With heartfelt appreciation and warm wishes,
xoxo Einar